The Twelve Days of Christmas

Adapted by Jillian Harker
Illustrated by Jane Swift

p

The Twelve Days of Christmas

On the first day of Christmas,
My true love sent to me
A partridge in a pear tree.

On the second day of Christmas,
My true love sent to me
Two turtle doves and a partridge in a pear tree.

On the third day of Christmas,
My true love sent to me
Three French hens, two turtle doves
And a partridge in a pear tree.

On the fourth day of Christmas,
My true love sent to me
Four calling birds, three French hens,
Two turtle doves and a partridge in a pear tree.

On the fifth day of Christmas,
My true love sent to me
Five gold rings, four calling birds, three French hens,
Two turtle doves and a partridge in a pear tree.

On the sixth day of Christmas,
My true love sent to me
Six geese a-laying, five gold rings, four calling birds,
Three French hens, two turtle doves
And a partridge in a pear tree.

On the seventh day of Christmas,
My true love sent to me
Seven swans a-swimming, six geese a-laying,
Five gold rings, four calling birds, three French hens,
Two turtle doves and a partridge in a pear tree.

On the eighth day of Christmas,
My true love sent to me
Eight maids a-milking, seven swans a-swimming,
Six geese a-laying, five gold rings, four calling birds,
Three French hens, two turtle doves
And a partridge in a pear tree.

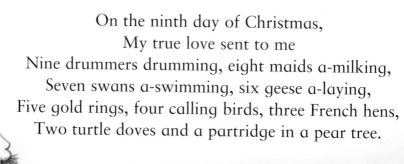

On the ninth day of Christmas,
My true love sent to me
Nine drummers drumming, eight maids a-milking,
Seven swans a-swimming, six geese a-laying,
Five gold rings, four calling birds, three French hens,
Two turtle doves and a partridge in a pear tree.

On the tenth day of Christmas,
My true love sent to me
Ten pipers piping, nine drummers drumming,
Eight maids a-milking, seven swans a-swimming,
Six geese a-laying, five gold rings, four calling birds,
Three French hens, two turtle doves
And a partridge in a pear tree.

On the eleventh day of Christmas,
My true love sent to me
Eleven ladies dancing, ten pipers piping,
Nine drummers drumming, eight maids a-milking,
Seven swans a-swimming, six geese a-laying,
Five gold rings, four calling birds, three French hens,
Two turtle doves and a partridge in a pear tree.

On the twelfth day of Christmas,
My true love sent to me
Twelve lords a-leaping, eleven ladies dancing,
Ten pipers piping, nine drummers drumming,
Eight maids a-milking, seven swans a-swimming,
Six geese a-laying, five gold rings, four calling birds,
Three French hens, two turtle doves,
And a partridge in a pear tree.

Ivy's Christmas Surprise

One snowy Christmas Eve, many years ago, there was a spoilt, little girl called Ivy.

"Can I stay up," she said to her daddy, "to see if Father Christmas is real?"

"But if he finds you awake," said Daddy, "he won't leave you any presents."

"He will," replied Naughty Ivy. "Anyway, I don't think he is real. It's only a story."

"Well, who leaves the presents, then?" called Ivy's mummy, from the kitchen.

"Daddy, of course!" grinned the cheeky, little girl.

"It's not me," laughed her dad. "Now, come on, Ivy – it's time all little girls were in bed!"

But Naughty Ivy wouldn't budge. Instead, she snuggled on the sofa between Mummy and Daddy.

"Oh let me stay up for five more minutes," she begged.
"But what if Father Christmas comes?" said Daddy, yawning.
"Won't you be sad when you don't get any presents?"
"But I will!" insisted Naughty Ivy. "You'll see!"

So, the clock ticked by and Mummy and Daddy dozed by the fir

Naughty Ivy sat quietly until midnight, then woke her parents with a yell.

"See!" she cried. "He's not coming, is he? I knew he wasn't real!"

Suddenly, there was a strange rumbling sound and then –
Father Christmas came down the chimney!

"Ho, ho... " he started to say and then he saw Ivy! "Goodness
me!" he spluttered, in surprise. "Why aren't you in bed?"

Naughty Ivy was shocked!

"AGGGH!" she screamed.
"You are real!"
"Oh dear, oh dear," tutted
Father Christmas, sadly, picking
up his sack. "This will never do!"
And he disappeared back up
the chimney!

Naughty Ivy began to sob.

"Daddy," she wailed, "please make him come back!"

"Get up to bed quickly, Ivy," called her father, looking up the chimney. "If Father Christmas sees how sorry you are, it might not be too late."

When Naughty Ivy woke the next morning, she felt very sad.
"There'll be no toys for me today," she said.

Then, she stopped and rubbed her eyes. Was that a stocking by
her bed? It was and it was bulging with presents!

"Hooray!" squealed Ivy. "Father Christmas changed his mind!"
"Yes," laughed Ivy's daddy, peeping round the door.
"But he said that next year, you'd better be in bed nice
nd early!"
"Oh, I will be, Daddy," smiled Ivy, happily. "And that's
promise!"

O Little Town of Bethlehem

O little town of Bethlehem, how still we see thee lie
Above thy deep and dreamless sleep the silent stars go by
Yet in the dark streets shineth, the everlasting light
The hopes and fears of all the years are met in thee tonight.

For Christ is born of Mary, and gathered all above
While mortals sleep the angels keep their watch of wondering
love
O morning stars together, proclaim the holy birth
And praises sing to God the king, and peace to men on earth.

How silently, how silently, the wondrous gift is given
So God imparts to human hearts the blessings of his heaven
No ear may hear his coming, but in this world of sin
Where meek souls will receive him still, the dear Christ enters in

O holy Child of Bethlehem, descend to us we pray
Cast out our sin and enter in, be born in us today
We hear the Christmas angels, the great glad tidings tell
O come to us, abide with us, our lord Emmanuel.